Book/Accompaniment CD

SOLOS
for the
TRUMPET
(CORNET)
PLAYER

With Piano Accompaniment

Selected and Edited by
WALTER BEELER

On the accompaniment recording:
JEANNIE YU and LAURA WARD
pianists

ED 2448-B

ISBN 978-1-61780-625-4

G. SCHIRMER, *Inc.*

DISTRIBUTED BY
HAL•LEONARD®
CORPORATION
7777 W. BLUEMOUND RD. P.O. BOX 13819 MILWAUKEE, WI 53213

www.schirmer.com
www.halleonard.com

CONTENTS

Pianists on the CD:
[1] Jeannie Yu
[2] Laura Ward

1. Theme and Variations

Transcribed by Walter Beeler

Marin Marais
(1656–1728)

Var. II **Allegretto**

Var. V **Più mosso**

2. Sonata Movements
from Six Sonatas for Violin

Transcribed by Walter Beeler

Willem de Fesch
(1687–1761)

Moderately
Allemande

Larghetto
Aria

3. Air
from Suite No. 3

Transcribed by Walter Beeler

Johann Sebastian Bach
(1685–1750)

4. Sonata Movements
from Flute Sonata in D Major

Transcribed by Walter Beeler

George Frideric Handel
(1685–1759)

Menuet

5. Le Tambourin

Transcribed by Walter Beeler

Jean Philippe Rameau
(1683–1764)

6. Allegro spiritoso

Transcribed by Walter Beeler

Jean Baptiste Senaillé
(1688–1730)

7. Finale
from Concerto for Trumpet

Franz Joseph Haydn
(1732–1809)

* Played ♪♫♫ etc.

8. Concert Rondo

Transcribed by Walter Beeler

Wolfgang Amadeus Mozart
(1756–1791)

9. Allegro

Transcribed by Walter Beeler

Franz Schubert
(1797–1828)

10. Cantique de Noël

Transcribed by Walter Beeler

Adolphe-Charles Adam
(1803–1856)

11. The Secret

Transcribed by Walter Beeler

Jean-François Eugène Gautier
(1822–1878)

12. Little Adagio

from *L'Arlésienne*

Transcribed by Walter Beeler

Georges Bizet
(1838–1875)

13. En fermant les yeux
from *Manon*

Transcribed by Walter Beeler

Jules Massenet
(1842–1912)

14. Andante and Allegro

Joseph Guy Ropartz
(1864–1955)

15. Petite pièce concertante

Guillaume Balay
(1871–1943)

ABOUT THE ENHANCED CD

In addition to piano accompaniments playable on both your CD player and computer, this enhanced CD also includes tempo adjustment software for computer use only. This software, known as Amazing Slow Downer, was originally created for use in pop music to allow singers and players the freedom to independently adjust both tempo and pitch elements. Because we believe there may be valuable educational use for these features in classical and theatre music, we have included this software as a tool for both the teacher and student. For quick and easy installation instructions of this software, please see below.

In recording a piano accompaniment we necessarily must choose one tempo. Our choice of tempo, phrasing, ritardandos, and dynamics is carefully considered. But by the nature of recording, it is only one option.

However, we encourage you to explore your own interpretive ideas, which may differ from our recordings. This new software feature allows you to adjust the tempo up and down without affecting the pitch. We recommend that this new tempo adjustment feature be used with care and insight. Ideally, you will be using these recorded accompaniments and Amazing Slow Downer for practice only.

The audio quality may be somewhat compromised when played through the Amazing Slow Downer. This compromise in quality will not be a factor in playing the CD audio track on a normal CD player or through another audio computer program.

INSTALLATION FROM DOWNLOAD:

For Windows (XP, Vista or 7):
1. Download and save the .zip file to your hard drive.
2. Extract the .zip file.
3. Open the "ASD Lite" folder.
4. Double-click "setup.exe" to run the installer and follow the on-screen instructions.

For Macintosh (OSX 10.4 and up):
1. Download and save the .dmg file to your hard drive.
2. Double-click the .dmg file to mount the "ASD Lite" volume.
3. Double-click the "ASD Lite" volume to see its contents.
4. Drag the "ASD Lite" application into the Application folder.

INSTALLATION FROM CD:

For Windows (XP, Vista or 7):
1. Load the CD-ROM into your CD-ROM drive.
2. Open your CD-ROM drive. You should see a folder named "Amazing Slow Downer." If you only see a list of tracks, you are looking at the audio portion of the disk and most likely do not have a multi-session capable CD-ROM.
3. Open the "Amazing Slow Downer" folder.
4. Double-click "setup.exe" to install the software from the CD-ROM to your hard disk. Follow the on-screen instructions to complete installation.
5. Go to "Start," "Programs" and find the "Amazing Slow Downer Lite" application. Note: To guarantee access to the CD-ROM drive, the user should be logged in as the "Administrator."

For Macintosh (OSX 10.4 or higher):
1. Load the CD-ROM into your CD-ROM drive.
2. Double-click on the data portion of the CD-ROM (which will have the Hal Leonard icon in red and be named as the book).
3. Open the "Amazing OS X" folder.
4. Double-click the "ASD Lite" application icon to run the software from the CD-ROM, or copy this file to your hard drive and run it from there.

MINIMUM SOFTWARE REQUIREMENTS:

For Windows (XP, Vista or 7):
Pentium Processor; Windows XP, Vista, or 7; 8 MB Application RAM; 8x Multi-Session CD-ROM drive

For Macintosh (OS X 10.4 or higher):
Power Macintosh or Intel Processor; Mac OS X 10.4 or higher; MB Application RAM; 8x Multi-Session CD-ROM drive